For all intrepid grandmas and grandpas
and the adventures and wisdom they'll share with their grandkids
—C.S.

For Lyn and Rob
—V.T.

The illustrations for this book were made with digital paint and watercolor.

Cataloging-in-Publication Data has been applied for and may be obtained from the Library of Congress.

ISBN 978-1-4197-4804-2

Text © 2022 Chris Santella
Illustrations © 2022 Vivienne To
Book design by Heather Kelly

Printed and bound in China
10 9 8 7 6 5 4 3 2 1

Abrams Books for Young Readers are available at special discounts when purchased in quantity for premiums
and promotions as well as fundraising or educational use. Special editions can also be created to specification. For details,
contact specialsales@abramsbooks.com or the address below.

Abrams® is a registered trademark of Harry N. Abrams, Inc.

ABRAMS The Art of Books
195 Broadway, New York, NY 10007
abramsbooks.com

Biking with Grandma

A "Wish You Were Here" Adventure

Written by
CHRIS SANTELLA

Illustrated by
VIVIENNE TO

ABRAMS BOOKS FOR YOUNG READERS • NEW YORK

I don't get to see Grandma Rose very much because she travels a lot for work. She goes on adventures and writes about them.

Now she's writing a book about great places to ride a bike. And this time, she's taking me along!

Mom and Dad made me promise to write from every place we visit. They didn't have to remind me!

Dear Mom and Dad—

Greetings from Alberta! Grandma and I are riding through the most beautiful mountains I ever imagined at Banff National Park. Across a meadow, we saw a grizzly bear. Grandma took a bunch of pictures . . . but we stayed a safe distance away. We took a hike to see a waterfall and slept last night at an old hunting lodge. Grandma had caribou for dinner. I think I surprised her when I asked for a bite—I kind of liked it!

Love,

Sam

P.S. Tomorrow we ride twenty miles. My butt isn't sore . . . yet!

Howdy, Partners—

Today I write from South Dakota. We're riding through the Black Hills, which feels like we're in the olden days. We're riding on the Mickelson Trail—it used to be a railroad, but now it's a bike trail. Pretty cool recycling! We cycled past bighorn sheep and pronghorn antelope—and bison, too. We also visited the Crazy Horse Memorial, which will one day be the biggest sculpture in the world. Crazy Horse was a brave warrior, and we learned how he protected his tribe, the Lakota, from U.S. soldiers who were taking their land.

Giddyup!
Sam

P.S. We drank sarsaparilla at a real saloon in the town of Deadwood. It tasted like spicy root beer.

Hey, shredders—

That's a word Grandma and I learned from our guide, Haley—it means you're a good mountain biker! We're now in Canyonlands National Park in Utah, riding a gnarly trail called the White Rim. We camp outside every night. There are hardly any other people around, and it's really quiet. The air is so clear here. I've never seen so many stars! Good for thinking.

stay rad,
Sam

P.S. You should see Grandma shred down the steep trails!

P.P.S. I heard a rattling noise this morning as we broke camp—it was a rattlesnake! Haley said they rattle to warn you of their presence. I was warned, and backed away slowly.

Hey, Parents—

Did you see any killer whales today? We did! We've been riding around the San Juan Islands in Washington State. We rode to the top of a mountain this morning—we had to walk our bikes part of the way because it was so steep. We made up rhyming songs to pass the time. Grandma's best was "Who cares about a hill/Riding down will be a thrill!" In the afternoon, we rented kayaks. That's when we saw the orcas. They're not really whales, but they're the largest members of the dolphin family. Who knew?!?

Your calf,
Sam

P.S. Calves are what baby orcas are called!

Aloha, Mom and Dad—

We arrived on the Big Island of Hawai'i on Tuesday, which is the largest island in the Hawaiian chain, and it's still growing. There's a mountain called Mauna Kea that's sacred to Native Hawaiians. It has snow on top and red-hot lava at the bottom (that's the growing part—when it hardens, it creates new land!). We started riding at a cattle ranch. I didn't think there'd be cowboys in Hawai'i—they're called paniolos! Yesterday, we rode to a huge hot spring that's heated by a volcano. This morning, we rode around a lava lake in the center of another volcano, called Kīlauea. Then we snorkeled near sea turtles.

Aloha,
Sam

P.S. Aloha means both "hello" and "goodbye" in Hawaiian!

G'Day, Mum and Dad—

Today I write from Down Under—way down under, because we're in Tasmania, an island south of Australia. We're riding through Cradle Mountain—Lake St. Clair National Park. We are seeing some fantastic animals: wombats, wallabies, and a platypus, which has fur and a duckbill—and it can lay eggs! We also saw Tasmanian devils. We took a hike yesterday to Dove Lake to see Cradle Mountain—it was reflected perfectly in the lake! Grandma was speechless, and you know that doesn't happen very often.

Peace out!
Sam

P.S. Our guide says Tasmania was connected to Australia 10,000 years ago, until the ocean levels raised due to melting ice.

chào bố mẹ—

That's Vietnamese for "Hi, Mom and Dad!" Our guide, Binh, has been teaching us how to speak Vietnamese. We started in a big city called Hanoi. It's very busy with cars and motorcycles and bikes. Very old buildings called pagodas are right next to big skyscrapers. There are rice paddies in the countryside, and farmers have water buffalo. Binh helps us have conversations with people we meet along the way. Grandma makes friends everywhere she goes.

Tạm biệt,
Sam

P.S. There are food carts everywhere. I loved a sandwich called a bánh mì, which has crunchy bread!

Konnichiwa, Okaa-san and Otou-san—

Greetings from Japan! We landed in Tokyo, which is home to 37 million people—more than any other city! But a few miles of pedaling put us in the countryside. We passed cherry trees with beautiful pink blossoms—so peaceful! Yesterday we stopped at a Buddhist temple and the priest showed us the koi pond. I was feeling a little homesick, but the smiling Buddha statues made me happy. Every night we went in the hot spring at our ryokan, a traditional Japanese inn. It was <u>very</u> hot, but Grandma said it was good for her old muscles.

Sayonara,
Sam

P.S. After dinner tonight, there was taiko drumming. The musicians let Grandma try. I don't think she was very good, but the musicians smiled.

Bonjour, Maman et Papa—

Yesterday, we started riding in the south of France. It smells so good here, like a bubble bath—Grandma says it's the lavender fields. Last night we got to play boules, which is like lawn bowling. Grandma showed me a secret way to throw the ball—did you know she was once a champion lawn bowler? We got to visit the building where Vincent van Gogh made some of his most famous paintings. The scenery that he painted looks the same today! Tomorrow night, we're going to stay in an old castle.

Au revoir,
Sam

P.S. The train we took from Paris was SUPER fast!

Buongiorno, Mamma e Papa!

That means "hello" in Italian, and it's what everyone says as we ride into the small villages of Tuscany! There are olive and fig trees everywhere. And grape vines, too! The food is excellent, though we didn't eat pizza. But we had something called bruschetta that was almost like pizza, and just as good. We took a cooking class at a farm and learned to make homemade pasta. Mmmmm! Some of the hilltop villages are 700 years old—imagine all that's happened inside those stone walls!

Ciao,
Sam

P.S. The ice cream is the best—they call it gelato.

Dumela, Mme, Rre—

We're in Botswana, where the national language is setswana.
Grandma and I have been pedaling on elephant trails! We're
on the savanna, and there are wonderful trees called
baobabs—some call them the trees of life. There are
animals everywhere: giraffes, warthogs, zebra, hyenas. "I bet there are lions watching
us," I said. "They'll be in trouble if they come after my grandkid," Grandma cried. Our
favorites are the elephants. We rode past a huge herd. One got mad and charged at
another. We couldn't believe how fast it was. "Would you save me from an elephant?" I
asked Grandma. "I'd try," she said quietly, giving the nearest the elephant the stink eye.

Go siame,

Sam

Buenas—

We are in Costa Rica now, where everyone says "pura vida"—pure life.
Grandma says that's because there's so much beautiful nature.
Yesterday, we saw a distant volcano that had lava flowing down its side.
Then we rode into the rain forest and went white water rafting. Grandma
and I helped our guide, Jorge, paddle. We saw toucans and a three-toed sloth,
and we heard howler monkeys yelling—they're scary loud. Tomorrow, we'll
bike to the beach. We might try to surf!

Con amor,

Sam

P.S. Grandma can do a great howler monkey impersonation. She made Jorge jump!

Dear Mom and Dad—

We're in Canada again, on Cape Breton Island. We're biking the Cabot Trail. Grandma read that it's one of the prettiest roads in the world. There are mountains on one side and the Atlantic Ocean on the other. Yesterday, a moose walked across the road in front of us. Moose are REALLY big! Pilot whales are even bigger, and we saw three this morning! There's lots of fiddle music here. We're going Highland dancing tonight. I'm not so sure about dancing, but Grandma said, "You're too shy, Sam. I'll show you how to have some fun!"

Gotta hit the road,

Sam

P.S. Grandma made friends with one of the fiddlers and sang a sad song while they played. It was so pretty!

Hi, Mom and Dad—

Almost home, but we have one more ride to go: the Blue Ridge Parkway in North Carolina. Grandma says lots of professional riders come here to practice because of the hills. I'm glad we came for the mountain views . . . and the hills aren't <u>too</u> hard. On our last day here, we took a break from riding and went rock climbing. Who knew Grandma was a climber? She's always surprising me. I'm sure going to miss hanging out with her.

See you soon!

Sam

P.S. The "blue" in the Blue Ridge comes from a chemical called isoprene that the trees release. Go figure!

Dear Grandma—

I can't believe that our trip is over! I miss our daily bike rides, but I have been getting Mom and Dad to ride their bikes with me around the park. (I'm a better rider than them, I think.) But most of all, I miss you—your smile, your funny stories, the way you played the taiko drums and zoomed down the mountain bike trail. Whoever thought I'd pedal all those miles? I didn't! But you encouraged me. Thanks for all the great memories.

Much love,
Sam

P.S. What are we going to do on our next adventure?!?